Published by Scholastic Inc.
90 Old Sherman Turnpike, Danbury, Connecticut 06816.

ISBN 0-7172-6821-7
Designed and produced by Bill SMITH STUDIO.

Printed in the U.S.A.
First printing, June 2004

Hold On to Your Hat!

A Story About
Humor

by **Jacqueline A. Ball**
illustrated by
Teresa Lester *with*
Duendes del Sur

SCHOLASTIC INC.

New York   Toronto   London   Auckland   Sydney
Mexico City   New Delhi   Hong Kong   Buenos Aires

*T*he wind whistled outside the castle where Cinderella lived with the Prince. Cinderella fastened her cloak as her mouse friends, Jaq and Gus, watched.

"Cinderelly going outside?" asked Jaq.

"Too cold! Too windy!" Gus squeaked.

"*I* need to get my new hat from the village," Cinderella replied. Her face was flushed with excitement. "I'm going to wear it at the ribbon-cutting ceremony for the new Royal Playhouse tomorrow."

*S*he twirled around and around. "It is nice to have such pretty clothes," she said happily as she remembered the clothes she once wore.

"My new hat is made of blue velvet and trimmed with pearls," she told the mice. "It matches the blue velvet gown I'll wear tomorrow."

There was a soft knock on her door. "Princess Cinderella?" a voice called politely.

The mice scurried under the bed. Beatrice, one of Cinderella's ladies-in-waiting, came in.

"The coach is waiting, Princess," Beatrice announced.

"Thank you," said Cinderella. "But why don't we walk instead?"

$\mathcal{B}$eatrice frowned. "Walk? But the wind is very strong, Princess. We might catch a cold."

"Nonsense. The fresh air and exercise will do us both good," Cinderella said.

So they walked down the steep hill towards town, clutching their cloaks to stay warm.

Along the way, everyone stopped to say
hello to Cinderella. Her old friends missed her
now that she lived in the castle.

"I miss them," Cinderella told Beatrice.
"I wish I could spend more time with them."

The signs read "BUTCHER", "MISTRESS FUSSENFEATHERS", and "HAT MAKER".

"*That* would be a bit difficult with your duties as a princess," said Beatrice primly. She raised her voice to be heard over the wind.

*I*nside the hat shop, they waited while Mistress Fussenfeathers went to fetch Cinderella's hat. There were many other hats on display.

"They're all lovely, but I can hardly wait to see mine!" Cinderella whispered to Beatrice.

"*I* hope you won't be disappointed, Princess," Beatrice warned. "There won't be time to make another one before the ribbon-cutting ceremony."

$\mathcal{M}$istress Fussenfeathers hurried back, holding a blue velvet hat trimmed with shimmering pearls.

"I hope this will do," she said anxiously.

Cinderella clapped her hands. "It's perfect!"

"It is quite beautiful," Beatrice agreed.

Cinderella tried on the hat, imagining how she would look wearing it the next day.

"I love it!" she told the hat maker. "Why, I don't even want to take it off!"

Mistress Fussenfeathers sighed with relief.

Cinderella was still wearing the hat as they left the shop. Outside, the strong breeze ruffled the back of her new hat.

"You'd better take that off, Princess," suggested Beatrice, "before it blows—"

Just then a powerful gust blew the hat right off Cinderella's head!

"Oh!" Beatrice cried.

"No!" Cinderella cried.

They watched the hat float away.

"It's gone," said Beatrice, shaking her head.

"It's not gone yet," Cinderella said firmly.

"Come on!"

They began to chase the runaway hat.
The butcher began to chase the hat, too.
So did the children and their dog.

Soon many people were trying to help
Cinderella catch her hat.

The wind stopped for a moment. The hat
started to drift down. "Hooray!" said Cinderella.

"*I*'ve got it, Princess!" the butcher called. But the wind whipped up again, blowing the hat out of his reach and swooping up some of his sausages. Then a blackbird grabbed the hat and flew away.

Cinderella gasped with laughter at the sight of her hat sailing along with the sausages.

Meanwhile, people kept joining the crowd. Soon it seemed as if all the townspeople were running with her.

The wind huffed and puffed.

One puff blew off the baker's hat. Another gust blew away the flower seller's banner.

The villagers tried to catch the flying things, but the wind blew them out of reach.

*T*he crowd chased Cinderella's hat out of the village and across a field, where a woman was hanging out her washing.

Whoosh! The wind blew her handkerchiefs off the clothesline.

"Come back here!" the woman shouted, joining the chase.

Now polka-dotted hankies floated alongside everything else. Beatrice clasped her hands in dismay, but Cinderella couldn't stop laughing at the silly sight.

Out of breath, the crowd finally stopped at a river. Cinderella's hat and the other items were floating just above the water.

At that instant the wind stopped, too. This time, it stopped for good.

Cinderella's laughter stopped, too. She watched in horror as her beautiful new hat fell into the river with a loud *kerplunk!* One by one, the other objects also fell in.

The fishermen cast out their lines and began to pull the things to shore.

*F*inally, one of the fishermen caught
Cinderella's hat.

Cinderella hardly recognized her hat. The cap was torn. Some pearls were missing. The blue velvet was soggy and dirty. Now the perfect outfit she had planned for the ribbon-cutting was ruined. She was upset and disappointed.

*W*hat would a princess do?

All of a sudden a fish jumped out of the hat. Surprised, Cinderella jumped, too. Then she began to laugh all over again.

Beatrice was shocked. "Princess, how can you laugh when your new hat is ruined?"

"My hat may be ruined," Cinderella said, "but look what fun we've had today. Anyway, laughing always makes me feel better. Just try it!"

Beatrice stared at the soggy items. A little smile crossed her face. Soon she was laughing, too.

"I lost my hat, but I gained something better," Cinderella announced to her friends. "The chance to see all of you and have fun!"

Then Cinderella invited everyone to the castle for refreshments.

The Prince joined them there.

"*I*'m sorry about your hat, but you'll look just as beautiful without it," the Prince told Cinderella.

"I can get another hat, but I can't get better friends than these," she said.

The End